BALLYTURK

Enda Walsh

THEATRE COMMUNICATIONS GROUP
NEW YORK
2015

Ballyturk is copyright © 2014 by Enda Walsh

Ballyturk is published by Theatre Communications Group, Inc., 520 Eighth Avenue, 24th Floor, New York, NY 10018-4156

This volume is published in arrangement with Nick Hern Books Limited, The Glasshouse, 49a Goldhawk Road, London, W12 8QP

All rights whatsoever in this play are strictly reserved. Requests to reproduce the text in whole or part should be addressed to the publisher.

Applications for performance by amateurs, including readings and excerpts should be addressed to: Nick Hern Books, The Glasshouse, 49a Goldhawk Road, London W12 8QP, tel +44 (0)20 8749 4953, *e-mail* info@nickhern-books.co.uk.

Applications for performance by professionals in any medium and in any language throughout the world should be addressed to Curtis Brown Ltd, Haymarket House, 28-29 Haymarket, London SW1Y 4SP, *fax* +44 (0)20 7396 0110, e-mail info @curtisbrown.co.uk

No performance may be given unless a license has been obtained prior to rehearsal. Applications should be made before rehearsals begin. Publication of this play does not necessarily indicate its availability for amateur performance.

This publication is made possible in part by the New York State Council on the Arts with the support of Governor Andrew Cuomo and the New York State Legislature.

TCG books are exclusively distributed to the book trade by Consortium Book Sales and Distribution.

A catalogue record for this book is available from the Library of Congress.

ISBN 978-1-55936-493-5 (paperback)

Cover photo of Cillian Murphy and Mikel Murfi by Richard Gilligan (www.richgilligan.com)

First TCG Edition, April 2015

The world premiere of *Ballyturk* took place at the Black Box Theatre on July 14th, 2014 as part of the 2014 Galway International Arts Festival. Produced by Landmark Productions and Galway International Arts Festival, it was subsequently seen at the Olympia Theatre in Dublin, the Cork Opera House and the National Theatre in London. The cast was as follows:

1	Cillian Murphy
2	Mikel Murfi
3	Stephen Rea
Voices	Eanna Breathnach, Niall Buggy, Denise Gough, Pauline McLynn
Girl	Orla Ní Ghríofa, Aisling Walsh

Director	Enda Walsh
Designer	Jamie Vartan
Lighting Designer	Adam Silverman
Sound Designer	Helen Atkinson
Composer	Teho Teardo

To Eamonn – the most fantastic Mr Fox
Thank you for all those worlds

Characters

1

2

3

A seven-year-old GIRL

No time. No place.

A very large room – too large.

Essentially it appears to be a one-roomed dwelling. There's a sleeping area, a toilet and shower area, there are old wardrobes, battered wall units and what looks like a single pull-down bed. The oddest thing is that all this furniture has been pushed against the two side walls making a large area in the middle where there is nothing but a tiny camping table (with a tablecloth) and two kitchen chairs (cushioned).

The back wall looks vast – its painted surface white and powdery to the touch. On this wall a large mustard curtain is drawn – where possibly a window is.

The two side walls are of similar colour and texture but these walls are covered with stacked furniture and drawings. From where we sit it looks like a child's drawings of people's faces and animals and buildings and maps and countryside…

There is something unquestionably rural about this dwelling. It is both comfortable and austere – clean and shambolic. Though it isn't pushed on first viewing – tonally everything is dark and pale.

But firstly – we're in darkness.

Music plays for some moments.

A light very slowly fades up on the face of a man in his mid-thirties wearing a 1970s red hurling helmet.

We'll call him 1.

Out of breath, aglow in sweat and 1 is desperately finishing something epic –

1. ....and dawn shining now. (*Slight pause.*) It warms the air around him and pushes back all that was yesterday. (*Pause.*) And in his mouth he tastes the drink from last night, beneath

his nails the dirt from Marnie's garden, in his jacket the smells of her new perfume, the dust of glass from her window. His eyes close and the noises he carries are churned into one another and pounding out now into the dawn. They crash over their hills and through the woods and down into the stream that runs through Ballyturk.

A breath in the darkness – 1 *barely flinches.*

Marnie Reynolds would be waking up to her burnt kitchen – she'd smell the smoke from beneath her new perfume and hear the embers and she'd know that it was him. In the dawn he is barely the man he was yesterday. Poisonous his envy. Inescapable his crime. And the air is whispering still – (*Slight pause.*) 'Larry Aspen has a knife. He will never see the full morning.'

A pause and silence now.

It's over.

1 *looks upwards.*

Nothing.

The sound of crisps being eaten. He then turns to his left –

– the lights go up on the whole space.

Standing very close to 1 is a man in his mid-forties dressed only in his underpants and socks – covered head to toe in talcum powder. He is sporting a fantastic ginger mullet – the talcum powder accentuating its redness.

This is 2.

He stops eating his crisps, saves a few and carefully folds them up into a tiny square. He unzips a small pocket in the inside of his underpants and places the crisps inside.

He looks back up at 1.

2.   I probably should have dressed.

1   (*cold*). I don't think that would have helped.

2. It caught me off-guard.

1. It happens sometimes.

1 looks down at the knife he's holding.

With a Dustbuster, 2 sucks up the embers around 1's feet. When he's finished, he stands up.

2. Have we eaten properly?

1. We should.

1 turns away and walks over to the stage-right wall with the knife. He stands by a chest of drawers. Inexplicably he hops twice like a bunny rabbit and mimes stabbing someone. Frightening himself, he quickly opens up the top drawer and throws the knife inside.

He takes the hurling helmet off – gives it a withering look – and places it on the chest of drawers.

2 sees this.

From a shelf, 1 takes down a clock. He begins to wind it slowly and the action of this visibly calms him.

2 meanwhile has picked up a red balloon (there are three other red balloons in the space). Over on stage left he's slowly flicking through a box of records (45s) in their white sleeves but without their covers. He does this with great concentration.

1's meditative clock-winding has been interrupted as suddenly he's seen something.

It is something invisible to us – something hovering in the air in front of him.

He holds his breath so as not to scare it. Without looking at the shelf – he slowly places back the clock.

BANG!

2 has burst the balloon he was holding. He continues to flick through the records.

*His breath still held and 1 really needs to breathe now –
his body's contracting a little – his face is straining.
There's nothing for it – he takes a sharp intake of breath a
little too loud.*

2's found the record he's been looking for.

*1 concentrates on that something in front of him. His hand is
primed, he widens his eyes – and reaches out in a flash and
grabs a fly.*

2 carefully checks the record for scratches.

*1, keeping the fly secret from 2, feels the sensation of the fly
in his hand. It is a huge momentous find – his brain and
heart may explode. Slowly he raises his hand to his ear.*

*2 does not hear – but we hear what 1 hears – the buzzing of
the fly – extremely loud.*

1 lowers his hand quickly and the sound cuts.

2 ceremoniously places the single on the record player.

*1 is unsure of what to do with the fly – he's excited/panicked.
He goes to show it to 2 but instinctively decides against it.
Maybe he should hold it in his mouth or his pocket –
suddenly he has a better idea.*

*He walks quickly to a small cuckoo clock on the stage-right
wall – opens it – and places the fly inside and shuts the
little door.*

The record blasts out ABC's 'The Look Of Love'.

1 stares at the cuckoo clock and backs away from it.

2 opens a wardrobe door.

*Fourteen seconds into the song and suddenly 1 turns and
rushes over and takes out a pair of trousers from that
wardrobe – 2 steps into the trousers while taking a shirt out
of the wardrobe. In one movement 2 is in the shirt – both of
them buttoning the shirt's buttons.*

1 *races across the space as* 2 *opens a drawer in a chest of drawers.*

1 *flings open another wardrobe and dozens of shoes topple out. He drops to his knees and tries to find a matching pair.*

2 *is trying on a succession of jumpers and cardigans very fast.* 1 *returns with a pair of runners.* 2 *steps into them and opts for a bright-yellow golfing jumper. Brand new he removes it from its cellophane wrapper and flings it over his shoulders.*

At 1:04 in the song, he's dressed. Good.

1 *races to the fridge as* 2 *races to a cabinet in the kitchen area.* 1 *returns with milk and two bowls – while* 2 *returns with two boxes from the Kellogg's Variety Pack and two spoons.*

They sit – open their cereals – pour the milk and eat – sharing each other's cereal every other mouthful.

They finish and tidy away the breakfast things back in the kitchen.

As they do this – 2 *is undressing* 1*. When he is down to his underpants he is ready to step into the shower – which he does. There's a half-door where he drapes his underpants over.*

1 *showers in a woefully weak shower.*

2 *does some stretches and golf swings (from somewhere he's picked up a golf club – a titanium-made 3 wood).*

At 2:40 in the song – the shower is over and 1 *steps out of the shower in an elasticated* Star Wars *beach towel that hangs over his shoulders. He dries himself, puts on his underpants and drops the towel.*

2 *covers him in talcum powder – firing it at him from washing-up bottles.*

They both run over to the dressing area. 2 *flings open the wardrobe and puts trousers on* 1 *as* 1 *opens the chest of drawers and takes out a red T-shirt.*

2 has put socks on 1 somehow and now runs over to the shoe wardrobe.

He throws open the door and tons of yellow ladies'shoes topple out. He tries to find a matching pair.

1 has a little rest.

2 runs back with a pair of ladies' shoes. 1 steps into them, walks around, hates them and kicks them off.

He goes to the freezer and takes out a pair of runners and places them on. Perfect.

The song ends as the alarm clock goes off.

2 saunters over to the alarm clock like a tiger (it was the one that 1 was winding) and switches it off – winds it for three seconds and puts it back on the shelf – when 1 is upon him fast and a little anxious –

1. So to finish what I started earlier –

2. Right.

1. – there was a terrible – whatyacallit – a terrible?

2. Wind?

1. No a terrible – it's a feeling – a sensation –

2. A draft?

1. It's like a draft but more overriding.

2. A breeze?

1. Less of a breeze and even more invisible.

2. A waft?

1. Tell me something of no importance and the word will come to me guaranteed.

2. Francie Lyon's head was twenty inches wider than his neck – from a distance he looked like a wandering yield sign.

1. Forebodance!

2. Foreboding.

1. Foreboding?

2. Foreboding.

1. A terrible foreboding!

2. Right.

   2 picks up another balloon.

1. And it was everywhere this feeling – not unlike the wind – but more surreptitious than the wind.

2. Like a draft?

1. It was exactly like a draft! And it came to me as I slept just then.

2. And it affected you?

1. It darkened me, yeah. You see I was having a dream about a small animal – the thing that we call a bunny rabbit.

2. A cuddly one?

1. He was lovely yeah.

2. Was he coloured cream?

1. No he was creamy white actually.

2. Awwwww.

1. So he was out shopping in the shops for groceries –

2. As rabbits do.

1. – and he had just taken a shopping bag out of his car when he heard a voice from across the street calling him – it was his brother.

2. Another bunny?

1. He came from a long line of bunnies.

2. Okay.

1. Our bunny – the creamy-white one – hopped across the road – the busy road –

2. Already foreboding.

1. I know, right!

2. Was he struck by a car!?

1. He wasn't no.

2. Was it a truck?

1. No.

2. Was he very nearly struck by a vehicle?

1. No he wasn't at all. He made it unharmed to the other side of the road – whereupon his brother pulled a knife on him and pushed it into his head. Out of nowhere, no reasoning at all, no history.

2. Well that's family for ya.

1. No sense to it but it seemed, you know –

2. Inevitable.

1. Exactly.

BANG!

2 explodes the balloon.

We've probably talked about this but it's worth having the conversation again. Is it at all possible – let's use the example of a bunny rabbit seeing as we're here already – though I could be talking about me or you…

2. Let's not talk about us.

1. Bunnies are a little more arbitrary.

2. They are.

1. Do bunnies definitely have legs by the way?

2. We decided on five.

1. Five?!

2. Yeah I know.

1. Is five enough?

2. I think so.

1. Anyway! Is it at all possible for a bunny to carry with them the full spectrum of characteristics at all times during the day as they hop about their business?

2. Absolutely it is!

1. Seriously?!

2. Oh definitely!

1. The thought of a bunny being innocent-kind-affectionate-generous-welcoming-shy-reserved-cold-calculating-devious-cruel-malevolent-murderous and savage all at the same time – it's a terrifying thought, isn't it?!

2. A malevolent bunny is terrifying, yeah.

1. I mean, how would you know?

2. How would you know what you were dealing with.

1. I don't think bunnies should be given that complexity.

2. No.

1. It feels like it might be stifling for something so fluffy.

2. You're right yeah.

1. Grand for us human beings but a little too tangled for an animal.

2. Human beings can cope with a little more complexity, all right.

1 (*like it's hilarious*). It is tiring, mind you!

2. Yeah it's exhausting – but to think if you were born a chair! And just how restricted and dull the life of a chair must be!

1. Right.

> 1 *slowly walks over to the cuckoo clock and the hidden fly.*

2. So really the luck to have been born a human being – to see what we say and to experience people and places and very occasionally moments of miracle...

> 1 *adopts a ridiculous pose where he has casually placed his ear against the clock.*

> *As he does this we hear the very loud buzzing of an angry fly as 2 yabbers on about stuff we thankfully can't hear.*

> 1 *removes his ear from the clock, the fly noise is cut and –*

...I mean it crushes me when I think what a wall must live through!

1 (*distant*). Right.

2. Just standing there! And yeah it serves a purpose and it has a stoic quality but nothing ever changes for a wall! Smaller things can get away with reserve but a wall looks terribly awkward in its silence!

> *Suddenly a loud muffled noise is heard behind the stage-right wall.*

1. Sshhhh!

> *They freeze and stare at the wall – and as they do we hear clearly two voices on the other side.*

VOICE 1 (*an old man*). And you saw Jimsy, you said?

VOICE 2 (*a young woman*). Oh I did ya?

> 2 *has grabbed the red hurling helmet.*

VOICE 1. And how did he look?

VOICE 2. He looked fuckin' terrible.

VOICE 1. 'Fuckin' terrible'? – Jaynee!

VOICE 2. Just like you imagine an old man would look riddled with cancer.

2 places the helmet back on 1's head.

VOICE 1. Ohh is he riddled?

VOICE 2. From head to toe he is.

VOICE 1. I thought it was only the left side of his brain.

1. Hello in there!

VOICE 2. Well it got in through his left ear –

VOICE 1. Right.

VOICE 2. – but then journeyed west –

VOICE 1. Okay.

VOICE 2. – only to travel south.

VOICE 1. My God.

VOICE 2. Whereupon it riddled him.

VOICE 1. He should have worn a hat.

1. That's what I was going to say!

VOICE 2. Did you eat that egg I gave ya, by the way?

VOICE 1. Oh I did yeah! Jesus it was divine! A magnificent yoke!

VOICE 2. You love eggs.

1. I love eggs!

VOICE 1. Oh I worship an egg. I do often daydream of changing shape like that of the Greek Minotaur but in chicken-form.

VOICE 2. Okay.

VOICE 1. Happily I would sit around laying eggs into my hand and eating them religiously. And although devouring one's unfertilised young may seem completely disgusting to some people, my conscience would be forever beaten by the promise of an eggy stomach!

VOICE 2. I'll bring you an egg from Drench's tomorrow so.

VOICE 1. Oh good girly!

1 hammers the wall.

1 (*calls*). Hello in there! Hello…!

There's no response.

2 is now holding the last two balloons pretending they're weights. 2 watches 1 – something's going to happen –

Is that a new jumper?

2. 'Tis-new-yeah.

1. Are you going to wear it like that?

2. Like what?

1. Like – over the shoulders.

2. I might do – I haven't decided.

1. It's good with your hair.

2. Thanks very much.

1. I wish I had better hair.

2. Hair's a great companion and level-headed too – to think what it has to put up with.

1. What's that?

2. Pushed from the inside so that what it shows on the outside is already dead.

1. Seriously?

2. Absolutely.

1. Imagine the will that takes. To continue growing all that time knowing that your dead bits are being manipulated into new life. I couldn't do it.

2. Me neither.

1. If the conditions were right, I might be able to do it.

2. Yeah if the conditioning was right, you might.

1. I might draw a picture of that image later...

2. That'd be lovely...

2 quickly gets to the back of 1 and holds him – as 1 collapses.

1 convulses violently/quietly.

The seizure stops after ten seconds.

His body now still – and 2 holds 1 for a few more seconds before letting him go.

1 looks at him. He takes off his helmet and hands it to 2.

1. Thanks.

2. Okay.

1. Isn't it time yet?

2. Lemme check...

1. No no no let me...!

2's walking to the cuckoo clock –

2. Don't be silly!

2 goes to open the little door but 1 slaps his hand away.

1. Let me, I said!!

2 looks at 1 and whacks him hard on the forehead with his knuckles.

It hurts – both of them.

2. Sorry!

1. Sure.

2. A little too –

1. – zealous.

2. Right – sorry!

1 and 2 walk away from the clock but 2 quickly doubles back and opens the little door.

The fly flies out and 2 swipes at it with the golf club a few times.

He throws the club to the side, claps his hands and crushes it.

A pause as they both feel the moment.

1 *and* 2 *look down at the dying fly on the floor – 2 quickly stands on it.*

Then –

1. What was that?

2. Dust.

1. I didn't know that dust buzzed.

2. It can do yeah.

A slight pause.

1. I didn't know it could grow wings.

The cuckoo shoots out of the clock and calls loudly three times.

On the third time, 1 *goes to the curtain on the back wall and holds the rope to pull it open.*

2 *picks up three darts and faces the curtain two metres from it.*

1 *opens the curtain with a –*

Whoosh!

Written in red-neon Celtic calligraphy, the word 'BALLYTURK' noisily flickers on. Underneath it are dozens of small drawn faces.

2 *closes his eyes and fires a dart into the wall.* 1 *checks where it stuck.*

(*Through a microphone.*) Larry Aspen.

2 *fires another dart at the faces.*

Joyce Drench.

2 whispers 'Cody Cody' over and over and fires his last dart.

Cody Finnington.

2. YES!

1 closes the curtains.

2 turns towards us, puts on the yellow jumper (it's tight) and composes himself.

He slowly raises his hand upwards. He's holding a comb.

1 cranks a large lever and the stage is plunged into darkness but for a small light on 2's face.

As 2 slowly combs his hair –

He stands on Moyne Street his heart paused, all his small yesterdays huddled around each other – for soon they would mean nothing – soon all his days would be scratched out – 'cause today would be the first day of his last days. Today the people of Ballyturk would make it so.

The world of Ballyturk is told almost like film noir – lights cut through the darkness and catch detailed glimpses of what 1 and 2 are creating in the moment.

1 is seen in the shadows.

1. Somethin' about that jumper and how he stands there expecting people to orbit his greatness has Larry Aspen itchin' to take his piece of him. Cody restin' a fag in his lips like he's suckin' the feckin' thing –

2. Larry.

1. Shockin' day, isn't it?

2. It is yeah…

1. Just when you tink it might –

2. – it doesn't yeah.

1. It's like it can't decide itself.

2. I know Larry, yeah.

1. Off to deliver a little present to Marnie Reynolds, Cody.

2. Ah that's nice.

1. I can't say I ever saw a yella jumper.

2. Haven't ya ever?

1. Never no.

2. Oh right.

1. Browns and blacks are more of what you expect round here.

2 (*narrates*). His grubby fingers twitchin' about Marnie's present.

1. Sorta-pops-outaya-that-jumper.

2. His polished shoes doin' a two-step on the kerb.

1. It's-sorta-you-not-you.

2. That smirk crackin' into a gape.

1. What the feck are ya wearin' yella for?!

2. Walk away.

1 (*calling after him*). I HATE FECKIN' YELLA!

2. Walk away from Larry with the jumper tighter around my body – the coins in my hand remindin' me of Joyce Drench's Emporium of Groceries.

1. Cody!

2. Walk through Ballyturk and the birds are flyin' from the woods.

   1 *opens a wardrobe and a corridor of light in which birds noisily fly –*

   They take to the rooftops and caw all manner of nonsense downwards. Can see them ahead outside Deasy's and they're feedin' on last night's chips. Nearin' them now and they scatter 'cept one. A fat bird jabs at a burger – his hate for me and my jumper taken out on that skinny slab of meat.

1. Feckin' yella!

2. They gather on the wires and look down as I walk onwards and into Joyce's with thoughts of a glass of milk back home and maybe a lovely Hobnob.

   Sound of a door 'dinging' open.

   A light slowly comes up on 1 standing high – he's slowly putting tins of peas onto a high narrow shelf full of tins of peas.

1. Her tiny feet on the ladder-steps and Joyce Drench is packin' away tins of peas. Her head full of last night's bingo, her agonising defeat to Marnie Reynolds and her own reliance on lime in lager. She hears him enter – the smoke on his breath visible before he is.

2. Mornin' Joyce.

1. Mornin' Cody.

2. The fridge in the back of her shop groaning and callin' me downwards. I stand tinkin' about my mottled life and lookin' at her yogurts.

1. And she starin' at his jumper like he's King F-in' Midas.

2. Any semi-skimmed milk?

1. Somethin' about those words, about that jumper – somethin' in how he stands there, in how he talks, narrows her little shop, cheapens it and marks her down as less than him. (*Slight pause.*) Behind the eggs!

2. Walk back with the milk and she's stood there in her pink slippers with scorn cut into her craggy face.

1. I never seen a yella jumper before – not somethin' you'd ever see – not common.

2. No not common.

1. Not normal in any sense.

2. Maybe-not-no.

1. What is it you have against brown, Cody?

2. I've nothin' against brown actually.

1. Brown's a perfectly good colour.

2. I know it is yeah.

1. It hasn't got the show of a yella but brown's a great base for a man –

2. Okay.

1. – as is whole milk. Sure what's semi-skimmed but the anaemic cousin to the full-fat…

2. Right well thanks Joyce!

1. From where I'm standin' I'm not hearin' thanks at all!

2. I walk away.

1 (*barks*). Not even close, Cody!!

Sound of a door 'dinging' closed.

2. Walk on –

1. Not close!

2. – and back out to Moyne Street with the semi-skimmed as a silent companion. The birds have brought the cats and the streets start packin' with the smell of kitty-cat and their endless keening. Walk over the cats with the birds divin' from the wires and snappin' at my new jumper! All is birds and cats and feathers and fur and what a curse to step out into this town…!

A cacophony of horrible sounds as 2 walks over the cats – and the birds peck holes in his unfortunate jumper.

And now from behind their windows I can hear them start over again. And they're spinnin' tales about me and the yellow jumper. Sniggerin' into cups of tea and draggin' up

other half-truths that I never stood up to before! If I could
find that voice and see those words and tell them how it was,
how it always is for Cody...!

1. Oh mother of shite!!

2. And Larry Aspen's stood bangin' on Marnie's door, clutchin'
   that little gift –

1. Whatcha wearin' yella for?!

2. Walk past and fast now!

1 (*hammering*). Come out and take a-look at dis Marnie-love!

2. I forget all thoughts of milk and biscuits –

1. A pressie, Marnie!

2. – and march with the town shovin' me t'wards the woods. To
   the woods – to the woods – to the woods!

   *A moment of rest and through the music – the sound of a
   breeze through the trees can be heard.*

   And hidden and safe now. Let that quiet sound take me there.
   (*Slight pause.*) My shoes in the soft floor and for a heartbeat
   it feels like I'm the only man alive.

   He takes out the ends of his crisps and eats them.

   But then –

   And that's when it starts. The jumper moves in on me. It
   squeezes around my skin and harder it pushes – and in doing
   so it begins to push up all this hate I have for the town of
   Ballyturk. It forms inside streams of sharp thoughts – till I'm
   shoutin' into the trees these years of trapped and swallowed
   gutless words! But trapped no more! For an hour I shout
   myself hoarse – and with each moment a better me – a
   stronger me!

1. All that hate for Ballyturk it rises from his throat and into
   the branches to somewhere safe it goes. But the birds are
   up there waitin' and listenin' and the birds will have their
   say...

2. And walk back through the woods with all my spite spat out
   – my body lighter for all of that. And soon to be back home
   with the biscuits and the not-too-full-fat-milk, Cody! Soon to
   be safe and plugged into ease…

1. But then.

2. And feck it then.

1. A black cloud sits down on Ballyturk.

   The sound of noisy birds gathering overhead –

2. The people are fallin' out of houses, their heads bent
   upwards –

1. – the birds are pickin' their time till he walks into town – and
   they speak those birds! They speak!

2. From the sky they speak all my hate.

   *1 has grabbed the microphone and mixed to make him sound
   half-bird –*

1. 'And what are those people but less than spit! Less than
   scum! And hardly born but cut from animals and reared as
   pigs! And ignorant fucking bits of muck – and uglier than
   sin the people of Ballyturk – and faces pulled from mash
   potato and bodies carved from gelatinous buckets of
   phlegm…!'

2. And the bad people of Ballyturk their heads bent me-wards –

1. CODY!

2. – they walk. They walk fast!

1. CODY!

2. The yellow jumper pins me down and unable to run they are
   on me now! And there is fists and boots and knives and teeth
   and tearin' of skin and pulling of innards and stamping and
   no no no no NO NO NO NO…

   *Music and sounds swell to noise. The space seems to shake
   until –*

*Everything suddenly stops and a single light snaps down on
2 as he looks upwards.*

*A sudden blast of air almost sucks him off his feet and for a
brief three seconds it is the most glorious release.*

*We crash back into the room's normal state – and how harsh
and bare everything looks now.*

Then –

1. Nice.

2. Thanks.

Blackout – for four seconds –

*Lights up with the alarm and 1 and 2 hop out of the pull-
down bed.*

2 walks over to the records.

1 is walking over to the alarm clock when he stops dead.

*There's a small flower (a marigold) in a flowerpot on the
shelf in front of the clock.*

He slowly approaches it like it was a bomb.

*2 has found the record he wants. He turns and sees 1 – he
sees the flower.*

1 takes the helmet off the chest of drawers and places it on.

*1 must reach around the flower to turn off the clock. He does
this.*

*The two men stand looking at the flower. How did it get
there?*

*2 turns away and puts on the record as 1 backs away from
the marigold.*

Suddenly Blancmange's 'Living On the Ceiling' is heard.

*Thirteen seconds into the song and the two men turn in to
one another and begin to dance a country-western two-step.*

They're good.

As it progresses, the formalities of the dance give over to new steps and improvisation.

At around 1:30, 1 convulses and the song suddenly stops.

Suddenly another very loud muffled noise is heard. They both look to the stage-left wall.

1. Sshhhh!

They freeze and stare at the wall – and as they do we hear clearly another two voices behind the wall.

VOICE 3 (*woman*). But ya look great – ya look absolutely wonderful!

VOICE 4 (*a young effeminate man*). Oh I feel wonderful. I feel invigorated actually!

1. Hello in there!

VOICE 3. It's like there's somethin' in ya – like a soul or somethin' coming out of your body.

VOICE 4. You know I think that's what was unlocked! Not that I didn't have a soul before the massage but the penetration was second to none.

VOICE 3. And from a woman – Jesus Christ?!

VOICE 4. I know, right! She wasn't a petite woman now.

VOICE 3. Was it Wags Mickles?

VOICE 4. In a certain light she was rather mannish looking and her hands were the hands of a strangler –

VOICE 3. But she realigned ya, nonetheless?!

VOICE 4. Oh she did yeah yeah yeah! Sure the health centre's a godsend!

1. There's a health centre!

VOICE 3. Well it's the only wheelchair ramp in town.

VOICE 4. Is it?

VOICE 3. The church's wheelchair ramp was torn up back in the winter.

VOICE 4. Jesus I never knew that.

VOICE 3. There was a terrible ground frost the morning of Collette Chinigan's funeral.

VOICE 4. Yeah right.

1 looks at the flower, 2 looks at the bed.

VOICE 3. Her three sons are ferocious alcoholics as you well know and apparently they were green on their feet as they carried their mother's remains out on their narrow shoulders. Sure poor Dinty Chinigan slipped on the icy wheelchair ramp – Collette came down on him hard – the casket's brass handles opening his head – like a fork being pushed into a boiled potato. To save on the cost of another casket they just lay Dinty's body on top of his mother's. Buried them both – like a Twix bar.

1 *(calls)*. Hello! Can you hear us?!

Silence.

It really does sound like there's someone there!

2 faces the microwave whose light is on – it pings loudly. He opens it and takes out two miniature steaming hot dogs.

2. So I don't want to build this up.

1. Build what?

2. What I'm about to say? I'm a little torn as to how I should start talkin' about it.

1. Why's that?

2. Because it may or may not be important.

1. Why does that matter?

2. You're right, it doesn't matter.

2 quickly measures the hot dogs and hands one to 1.

1 *eats it in a second.*

I had a dream about your bunny rabbit just then.

1. Seriously?

2. Deadly serious.

1. The five-legged one?

2. All bunnies have five legs.

1. So what happened?

2. Well it was before he went shopping for groceries, before his stabbing at the paws of his own brother – it was the morning of that same day.

1. How did you know it was that day?

2. It had that foreboding you talked about.

1. Forebodance.

2. Foreboding.

1. Foreboding?

2. Foreboding. It had that forebodance.

1. Foreboding.

2. Right.

1. So what was he doing?

2. He was at home brushing his teeth in his bathroom. His wife was sitting on the toilet and telling him all the things he needed to buy from Drench's.

Unconsciously 1 *has taken off the helmet and handed it to* 2.

1. Was she a rabbit?

2. No she was a woman.

1. Right.

2. You could tell they had a wonderful marriage just by how she was listing all the food they needed.

1. A lot of carrots?

2. Masses of carrots. And although it was a perfectly normal scene of a woman sitting on a toilet talking to her rabbit husband about vegetables – it already had a gathering darkness about it.

1. Bigger than what happened to him later? (*Makes the stabbing motion.*)

2. It was something to do with me and you, I think.

A pause.

1. Feck it, I don't feel well...

2. How'd ya mean?

1. I feel funny.

    2 *quickly places the helmet back on* 1.

2. Well sit down!

1. I don't want to sit!

2. Stand then.

1. Standing's not helping!

2. You could crouch.

1. Am I breathing any differently?

2. You're using your nose and mouth.

1. Right...

2. At the same time.

1. Okay...

2. Excessively. It's doing odd things to your face.

    1 *retches.*

1. My hand's shaking!

2. You're making it shake!

1. I'm making this one shake but this is being shook by something else.

2. By what?!

1. By fear! What d'you tell me that dream for?!

2. I didn't know you were scared of bunnies!

1. It isn't the bunnies!! If even in sleep we're talkin' the same thing – where's the space?

2. What ya mean?!

1. Sleep is freedom!

2. Freedom from what!? Why would you use that word…!?

2 slaps 1 in the face, hard.

1 immediately calms. He looks at his hand.

1. It's stopped.

2. It's normal to feel nervous when you've lost yourself, it can happen but it passes.

1. Right. Thank you.

2. Sure.

1 takes off his helmet.

Then –

1. How many other things have wings that I didn't know had wings?

2 doesn't answer.

I thought we knew everything there was to know. (*Slight pause.*) There was that story you told me once about that boy who'd seen a small cloud out on a lake – and it was in the shape of his sister – and he rowed out there towards her. He rowed with their past falling away behind him. (*Slight pause.*) He's sitting in a bath and his hands are holding the soap – and she's across from him singing something – and much later and through leaves and their hands are moving towards berries – and sitting then and eating those berries. And the two of them playing – and falling asleep then in a car – and asleep still and lifted and laid down together in the same bed and just barely awake and already talking fully to one another. (*Slight pause*.) He rowed that boat towards that image of her standing there – and closer – and of course not her – and her image not made up of cloud but something else, you said – and you said how that something else 'buzzed' – how its 'wings' moved it over the water towards him and the boat – and when that boy stood up and went to hold her – it was 'flies' was the word. (*Slight pause*.) Don't you remember saying all that? Saying that word. (*Slight pause*.) So that's what it was.

2. What?

1. 'It' – earlier.

2. It was dust.

A pause.

1. It feels like we may be less of what we were in a place we don't know wholly now. (*Slight pause*.) Do you feel that way?

A slight pause.

2. Barely.

1. 'Barely' is enough.

A pause.

2. So ya ready?

1. Okay.

2. Go.

   1 *starts listing Ballyturk people as* 2 *takes on their image*.

1. Larry Aspen. Jimsy Behan.

   Music.

Suzy Clutch. Nags Mickles. Boxer Brady. Phyliss Brady.
Tina and Tony Brady. Father Garrington. Dinty Chinigan.
Barbara Muffing-Field. Lexy Stafford. Honey Chasty.
Clifford Cleary. Marnie Reynolds. Big-Mick Langley.
Smidgee Coates. Nana Coates. Cody Finnington. Ferdy
Oppington....

*1 continues to call out names we don't hear as 2 continues to
pose as these people.*

It is endless.

Sad.

After thirty seconds of this, the cuckoo clock sounds.

*1 and 2 go to the clock and look at it. On the third call, 2
turns and goes to the curtain and opens it.*

*The music continues as 1 throws the three darts into the
faces and 2 calls their names through the microphone (we
don't hear him).*

*1 turns to us as 2 closes the curtain and pulls the lever – a
single light coming down on 1.*

*1 shoots up his hand. He's holding a large pair of women's
spectacles. He looks up at his hand and it's starting to shake
again.*

She stands on Moyne Street... (*Stops.*) I can't.

2 holds and calms 1.

Sound of a door 'dinging' open.

*A light comes up on 1 standing high – he's slowly putting tins
of peas onto a high narrow shelf full of tins of peas. He's
taken on Joyce Drench.*

Her tiny feet on the ladder-steps and Joyce Drench is packin'
away tins of peas. Her head full of last night's bingo, her
agonising defeat to Marnie Reynolds and her own reliance
on lime in lager. She hears her enter – the scent in the air
visible before she is.

2. Mornin' Joyce.

1. Mornin' Marnie.

2. Some bingo last-night-all-together-wasn't-it?

1. 'Twas, yeah.

2. I was only saying that to Larry when he popped inta me this mornin' to make plans for our special-evenin'-dis-evenin'. You might be able to detect the new perfume that Larry purchased as a little present for me.

1. Perfume right.

2. It's called, 'Just Maybe' – and I tink that's a very appropriate name for what me and Larry might accomplish tonight. I'm talkin' about a delicious dinner in The Rusty Anchor in celebration of Cody's mauling – followed by a midnight stroll by the stream – and who knows – maybe an ol'-fumble-in-da-woods!

1. What is it you need, Marnie?

2. When your perfume wafts in front of you a course that could navigate the most miserable of towns - - the only thing in need of benefaction is the interior.

1. And what's that then?

2. A packet of Polos. Thanks Joyce!

1. From where I'm standin' I'm not hearin' thanks at all!

2. I walk away.

1 (*barks*). Not even close, Marnie!!

Sound of a door 'dinging' closed.

2. Walk on –

1. Not close!

2. – and back out to Moyne Street with the Polo mints as a silent companion. Ballyturk lurches in silence – the buildings slumped against one another like five-day-old drunks – they

turn me in on myself and have me recallin' those romantic words shared between me and Larry that very mornin' –

1. People have said that your scent could rejuvenate the most fetid of toilets – like your floral fragrance was regurgitated from the mouths of flowers and spat onto your delicate neck.

2. Thank you, Larry.

1. But travelling on my travels – I happened upon a lady shop and purchased that bottle of perfume – on the off-chance that if I gave it to you outta respect and love – that after a meat supper in The Rusty Anchor – we could stroll hand in hand through the woods over the hills and allow our passion to create new languages for themselves – if you get my meanin', pet.

2. I walk through Ballyturk with Larry's words stuffin' my body with butterflies – curtains start twitchin' and whispers start knittin' together until the air invisibly fills with Larry and me, me and Larry. The birds awaken from their fill of Cody's jumper and caw all manner of derision downwards – but all this carries me even higher! For there's passion and possibility in them hills – there's life above the grey of Ballyturk, surely!

1 (*distant*). Aren't you smellin'… lovely, Marnie?

2 turns and sees that 1 is by the flower – he's staring at it.

2. Well that's awfully cheeky of ya, Ferdy Oppington!

2 waits for 1 to respond with a line.

1, facing the wall, leans his head against it. He's exhausted/bewildered.

2 is left to continue with the conversation himself – playing both parts.

Aren't you smellin' lovely, Marnie? Well that's awfully cheeky of ya, Ferdy Oppington! *Where is it you're off ta, love?* I thought I might take a trip to the health centre and get myself a massage, actually. *There's a woman who does that down there, is there?* She's a form of woman, yes – by all accounts she wouldn't be the most feminine of women and yet she can reduce a seized back into a pound of putty in minutes!

Suddenly 1 *crashes his head against the wall.*

Smellin' you right now, Marnie – and picturin' you bein' pounded by that She-Goliath – has sent my thoughts all a-skitter! I am aware of your emotional attachment to Larry Aspen...! Are you though?! *I am!* Are you sure, Ferdy?

A continuous high-pitched tone begins – low.

Your adhesion to that bedlamite is the most unnatural thing to surface in Ballyturk since that memorable afternoon when Clifford Cleary eloped with that pony! The whole town's sayin' it, Marnie – you deserve a better man!

Take a hold of your faculties, Ferdy!

1 *has turned to look at* 2 – *his forehead's bleeding. The tone raising in volume –*

The mind is a thunderous place – with all manner of dreams and wants and half-notions and clouded thoughts. (*Beginning to shout.*) Look at you there – stood up by trousers and shirt – but inside – inside a calamitous vessel of frogs you are – a vessel adrift on a sea of thoughtless, unanswerable questions! Are you listening...?

Suddenly a huge hydraulic noise – the sound of cracking.

Music

The lights revert to the room's normal state as we watch the back wall slowly tear away from the two side walls.

Where it was joined to these walls – the wallpaper rips – power cables spark aggressively – water pipes buckle and spray water.

The two men stand frozen.

*The wall continues opening and out into a beautiful blue
light – onto a small hill of green perfect grass – into what
must be the outside.*

*The wall falls onto this grass and we're looking at someone
standing on the hill.*

As he looks up – the music swells.

He is a man in his sixties dressed in a darkish suit.

We'll call him 3.

He slowly walks towards the two men.

*He steps into the room and the two men both take a step
backwards.*

*The music is gaining in volume and swirling now – 1 and 2
covering their ears to block the noise.*

3 smokes.

Silence – 1 and 2 are stunned.

Then –

3 (*about the cigarette*). Hope you don't mind. Terrible habit.
Been smokin' so long my right hand doesn't seem natural
without a cigarette in it. It seems undressed – a little bit
useless – or lazy – just hangin' there at the end of my wrist –
ageing a little bit faster than the rest of my body – so when
it's not functioning – when it's without a cigarette – it looks
a little idle and slackened. This hand – the left one – I'm
less critical of – I hardly think about it to be honest – I
imagine it's very happy that it was grown on the left side.
It's got the quieter existence of the two – a hand with pretty
much little functionality – it gets to laze about on desks and
tables and arms of chairs and legs of loved ones – and when
it's brought into life it's simply there to make shapes, to
express, to dance and ponce about. It must talk when it's
holding the right hand as it lies in bed at night and it must
taunt the right hand about havin' been dealt the easier hand,
so to speak. How exhausting to be writing and opening and

turning and prising and picking and poking and then the bloody wiping! – and then to be listening to my scorn almost every other hour because for all its action I am not in the least bit thankful to this right one because it's not of any use to me unless it's holding a cigarette as it is now! (*Slight pause.*) It seems unfair to focus and judge that which was born to work harder than the other one but which one has the fuller more colourful life but the right one, the doer of things... can I sit down?

2 looks at 1.

They both walk quickly and set up the small table. There is some business as there's only two chairs.

2 scans the furniture for something approaching the right size to sit on as 3 and 1 sit at the table.

2 finds what looks like a metal safe. He begins to push it over to the table. This takes all his strength and a considerable time. 3 and 1 watch him bursting blood vessels (at one point he stops for a drink) and inching the safe closer and closer.

He finally gets to the table and sits on the safe.

A pause as the three just sit.

Well this is nice! (*Slight pause. To* 2.) Do you have any tea?

2. We do yeah.

A slight pause.

3. Would you like to make some?

2. Not really no –

3. No you don't understand...

2. – it's not teatime yet! It will be soon and when that comes...

3. Make me a cup of tea.

2. Right.

3. Would you?

2. I'm thinking.

A pause.

Okay yeah.

3. Good man.

A pause as 3 stares at 2.

2. You want me to make the tea now!?

3. Yes I'd like you to make me a cup of tea directly after I finish talking – make us all a cup of tea. That's three cups of teas I would like you to make in three separate cups. (*Slight pause.*) Finished.

2 hops up and walks towards the kitchen area.

And what d'you have for snacks!?

1. We have hot dogs.

2. We have biscuits with tea!

1. We also have biscuits that we have with our teas.

3. Fix us a selection of biscuits that we can dunk into our teas.

2. Right.

2 turns and gets to work.

1 just stares at 3.

3 turns to him. From his pocket he hands 1 a little scrap of toilet paper.

1 wipes the blood from his forehead.

3. You're much older than I thought you'd be, you know.

1. Really?

3. Yeah you are – much.

1. Oh.

A long pause.

Then –

3. People grow up fast – apparently that's a tragedy but I've never seen it that way myself because of the way things are with me. There are only ever two pictures – the face then and the face now and it's interestin' to see what has stayed as is – the eyes, the bones around the eyes, the chin – and what has changed – what has been altered by wear and tear or by familial strains – to grow into your parent's face – to be pulled into the face of your father or mother and to follow as they followed their parents' faces – to be led by the nose that is no longer your nose but your father's nose, you get me? Do you have mirrors here?

1. Just the one.

3. Well one's more than some and some don't even have mirrors – so at least you've seen how you've aged – though it's impossible to gauge that as time inches by – but you've seen at least your reflection and maybe you notice small changes weekly – have you?

1. What do you mean by 'weekly'?

A slight pause.

3. Look all you need to know is that you've got older – you're no longer the you you were – and you are not yet the man your father is – or was. D'you have hobbies?

1. We like to listen to music and dance. I like to draw things.

3. What things?

1. Whatever I see in my head.

He gestures to his drawings on the walls.

3. This – Ballyturk?

1. Yeah. All the people there, all their houses and the places they shop – and the grey roads and the fields and woods and the stream through town and the birds and cats and… everything.

A slight pause.

3. I collect things. That's what I'm here for.

2 rushes over with three cups of tea and places them down.

He goes back to the kitchen and from a concealed area he lifts up a selection of biscuits arranged into a massive pyramid (three foot high).

2 carefully carries it over to the table and places the pyramid on the table. 3 is hidden behind it.

2 sits down on the metal safe with his own cup.

1 and 2 stare at the biscuits.

2 reaches out and inches a chocolate finger out of the pyramid (Jenga-style).

1 grabs a hold of a pink wafer and painstakingly eases it out. Success. He almost smiles when –

The pyramid collapses in a heap.

Suddenly a very loud muffled noise is heard behind the stage-left wall.

Sshhhh!

The old man from next door can be heard.

VOICE 1. Well speaking personally – I never really trusted my body, do you know what I mean by that?

The woman behind the other wall answers him –

VOICE 3. Oh-God-yeah-absolutely-I-know-exactly-what-you-mean!

VOICE 1. I always felt my body was followin' me around sort of.

3. Like a stranger, d'you mean?

VOICE 1. More like a friend I had once been close to but am no longer.

3. Aye I see.

1 and 2 are shocked that 3 can talk to them.

VOICE 1. You do?

3. Absolutely I do. As a younger man my relationship with my body was a lot easier than it is now – sure now it's like walkin' about in an old suit.

VOICE 1. It's a terrible waster the body.

VOICE 3. It can eat food, mind you!

3. But sure it even discards that.

VOICE 1. Unless you're Fat-Grainne-Packer –

VOICE 3. – a woman who's yet to surrender to the motions of the bowel.

VOICE 1. It can be a useful form of transport – I'll give the body that.

3. In the early days it is.

VOICE 1. Exactly – in the early days.

3. Degradable is what the body is.

VOICE 1. Disembodiment is what I dream of.

3. Why can't the head give up?

VOICE 3. Because it's in competition to stay on top of the body!

VOICE 1. The head is a torturer!

3. Why not die?

VOICE 1. Sure isn't that what we're busy doin' here!?

VOICE 3. Life gets in the way – people say that.

3. Aye, people do say that.

VOICE 1. People are fond of sayin' all manner of…!

A pause.

Blackout – for eight seconds –

Lights up with the alarm sounding and 1 and 2 wake up and hop out of their bed – the table, safe and chairs are gone.

They look at 3 who is already walking towards the alarm clock, eating a Marietta biscuit.

He finds the golf club leaning against the wall.

He places the clock on the floor and looks down at it screaming up at him.

With the golf club he lines up his shot. 1 and 2 slowly step out of the way.

As 3 draws back the club – the alarm suddenly cuts.

The jazz classic 'Time After Time' (Cahn/Styne; Chet Baker's version) plays warmly in the space.

3 begins to sing the first few lines of 'Time After Time' through the golf club.

He then sees something on the floor beneath him.

He sings another couple of lines.

He bends down and picks up the dead fly and holds it in his hand.

He sings another line.

He gently closes his hand.

He sings another few lines.

He raises his hand to his own ear – the sound of the fly buzzing loudly as it drowns out and cuts 'Time After Time'.

It's come back to life.

3 lowers his hand and lets the fly free.

Then –

3. I wonder do they know how brief their life will be? You know, whether it's somethin' they're thinking about as they grow inside that shell of theirs – is it somethin' they can ever imagine? Is it passed down from their parents and lies inside

them – and those broken images of the outside world passed down also and grown over those days as they grow inside. And they can hear surely the world outside – the incredible sounds – and how do they match what little they know with what actually is? What version of life are they making up inside those little homes? And maybe that's why the fly arrives out so noisy and feverish – it joins his brothers and sisters and they fly in hordes to start with – but the world they see is so much larger and quickly they're led by the instinct, by the breeze, by the need to discover things alone, by the knowledge that their time is so short. Outside and flying over and through something that seemingly has no order 'cause all is textures to them up there. There's a breeze that holds them and underneath is grass or maybe sand or rock turned into road – and there's peculiar-shaped bushes and trees – and each tree singular – each with its own needs, its own particular life – and yet all wanting to commune with other plants or animals – wanting to populate the world with its particular shape and colour and kind. From one season to the next a million flies grow from just a few and they fly over a landscape itself competing for more life, for time, for legacy. (*Slight pause*.) Did ya give each other names by the way?

The flies noisily disappear.

1. No.

3. And why not?

1. I don't know why.

3 (*to 2*). Can't ya remember deciding that?

2. No.

3. Did ya know I would come back?

A slight pause.

2. Maybe once I did.

3. But you'd forgotten. Everyone does. Everyone does.

He looks at 1's drawings on the wall. He then calls him over.

1 *goes to him and* 3 *faces him in front of the wall.*

2 *stands on the far side of the stage, isolated.*

What do you see when you speak about Ballyturk – do you imagine people's faces and homes – can you see them?

1. I see him as them – I see the drawings as the places – sometimes I see nothing but the word.

3. Because none of it's real – before the fly, before me.

1. Only inside our heads it is.

3. And that's enough for you?

1. I don't understand what you're asking.

3. Right.

A pause. Then –

Everything you've imagined – it is. All life. It's out there. Everything.

Like a light has gone off in him – 3 *visibly fades. He looks spent – older now.*

He looks over at the flower on the shelf. He opens the top drawer in the chest drawer and takes out the knife.

He goes to the marigold and quickly slices at the stem but it remains standing.

He fires the knife into the top of the chest of drawers.

He carefully picks the marigold off the stem – he's cut it beautifully.

He places the marigold in the buttonhole of his jacket.

He begins – maybe talking to himself –

There's a man and he wakes alone. His eyes open and he's conscious of his first breath, of his first movement, of his first thought which may be of food or may be to shuffle himself to his bathroom and relieve himself. And those first beginnings lie on top of twenty-three thousand mornings that

have passed where he has aged invisibly, definitely – where
he carries half-remembered bits of his life, of the people he
has met and hated and loved, of his brothers and sisters who
were once his world and now only exist to make him feel
older. He carries a billion pictures of life that have no
consequence to him and a few pictures which will always
haunt or please him. He's made from purpose and mistake
and controlled by the movement of this planet around a star
– yet in the second he's led by some great need or some little
urgency. Only occasionally he's conscious that around him
life is beginning and ending to the beat of time – that
millions of others are walking in the exact same moment that
he is – are travelling with the same purpose but with singular
histories – but travelling nonetheless with the same basic
need – to keep on living. How unremarkable and how faintly
unique to wake and walk in this way – with doors pushing
open into a sky bizarrely blue and giving to us systems of
weather, shaping us with forever-movable seasons. And too
hard it is to think how rain is made – how the sun can push
light through darkness – and what it is that holds us up here
imperceptibly in space – that man stands and walks in life as
it is now – with geographies to navigate – with journeys to
his wife, to his work, to lunches, to beaches, to churches, to
secret meetings with potential lovers, to parks, to other parts
of the village, or town, or city, or countries even. A lifetime
of walking distances in the vain hope of making things that
bit more fulfilling – of packing his time with experiences
some of which will change him greatly and others with no
consequence other than wasting a little more of his life. And
to stand there in the magnificence of this world with all these
animals and plants and trees too many to ever imagine
clearly – and standing with the you as was made – in a life
that is so chaotically structured by nature – to continue living
– to remain upright and to be able to carry on searching for
something other than what you have – some love or money
or experience or cat or cake or son or anything at all –
something which makes you continue without the
mindfulness of it all ending at any moment – for everything
is here and we are here to lay down legacy – to give life

purpose by reaching its edge. (*Slight pause*.) And it's time
for you two and for what you've made – time for one of you
to walk away and into your passing. In leaving you're giving
shape to life – some design and purpose for being what you
are – for this is the order that all life demands – (*Slight
pause*.) it needs a death.

A long pause.

3 is finished.

Then –

I can't see the start of my life to figure out how I've come to
this… this work. (*Slight pause*.) You give me a choice of
biscuits – I give you a choice as to which one of you will
step outside, walk the twelve seconds to me and die.

*He takes his packet of cigarettes from his jacket pocket.
There's one left.*

It's all been said. By me, at least. (*Slight pause*.) Right.

The music he enters to – returns now.

*He turns around and walks out of the room and onto the
grassy hill outside.*

*He stands there and the warm sun catches his face in profile
as he places the cigarette in his mouth.*

The wall rises noisily back up.

It crashes back into position – the music cutting abruptly.

*The two men locked inside their room once more – turn and
look at each other.*

Then –

*– the turntable begins to spin again, the arm and needle
moving into position and onto the record.*

*They stand across the space listening to the needle crackling
on the vinyl – waiting and expecting Blancmange to play
once again.*

Suddenly Yazoo launches into 'Situation'.

On 0:10 the two men race in opposite directions. They rifle through a chest of drawers full of marbles and table-tennis balls – that scatter across the floor.

They both find a skipping rope on 0:20.

On 0:25 they both begin to skip like professional boxers.

On 0:34 they throw their skipping ropes to the side.

2 takes off his shirt, grabs some suspension flexible cables attached to the left wall and begins some vigorous suspension training.

Meanwhile on the right wall, 1 has wrapped a canvas belt around his backside. He pushes a button and it begins to vibrate while he brushes his teeth.

On 1:02, 1 gets out of his vibrating belt, takes off his T-shirt and begins his own suspension training – while 2 has finished his and gets on an old stationary cycle machine (bolted to the wall) and cycles fast. As 2 cycles he's peeling mandarins and popping them in his mouth.

On 1:25, 2 races over and gets into the vibrating belt as 1 gets on the cycling machine.

All this time and their minds are racing with what 3 has left in the room – perhaps the exercise will expel these thoughts of life and death.

On 1:47 the two men finish their exercise.

1 grabs two spray-on deodorants from the right wall and 2 grabs two Remington electric razors from the left wall. They look across the space and suddenly race towards each other.

The deodorants and electric razors are attached to super-resistant elastic cables.

The two men just about meet in the middle where 2 shaves 1 and 1 deodorises 2 – in this manner they spring back and forth from their walls until –

– at 2:23 they and Yazoo stop.

2. So to finish what I started earlier – it's impossible to second-guess what hair will do – and although it gives me great pleasure – it's living and dying at a ferocious rate – it's an awful shame that some are regarded as hair solely.

1. Like Lexy Stafford.

2. A pioneer who polishes his crown as much as he does his boots – a man whose head caught fire on All Souls' Day and was eventually put out on Christmas Eve.

1. Honey Chasty.

2. A badly named glutton of a woman whose matted hair sat in the corner of The Rusty Anchor smelling of cheese and groaning.

1. Little-Mick Langley.

2. A balding midget who roamed Delaney's Field looking like a friendless football in winter.

The cuckoo clock suddenly sounds. Saved by the bird and 2 is already heading for the darts.

Hair's a cunning temptress all right – more often than not I feel like a fool to the follicle.

2 opens the curtain –

– the Ballyturk sign barely flickers on.

2 throws the three darts quickly in succession.

He quickly cranks the lever – grabs 1 and throws him into the spotlight.

Do it!

Then –

1. I'm too scared to talk.

2. Then don't.

1 *pulls the lever back and the space is lit back up.*

Go on.

A pause.

1. Bits and pieces of the almost forgotten – pictures I thought that were stolen from Ballyturk – where before they could never have been mine – now that man's face is knittin' them all together. What must be sand is on a seat – what must be the sun is shining through a window – and a small jaw chewing something sticky – of teeth almost being pulled from gums and fingers passing over the seat and through the sand – and bare feet dusted too and a body not yet broken by this room – it sits all happy in the back of a car – it's made still from what was before, by the sun, by the running, by the 'beach' is the word – and moments from sleep were it not for this sugar being chewed into my mouth. My mouth. (*Slight pause.*) It was mine. (*Slight pause.*) And I'm not in Ballyturk, not in any place we made – beyond the car window all is bleached by this light – there must be a street or shops out there – there could be car noises or sounds of the real countryside even. The light buckles and his face looking in at me – and I'm no longer there with the sun but somewhere else – and moving fast with him driving in front – and what could have been trees and what might have been real clouds – and what certainly is colour is passing me with that man's voice telling me to be quiet! Did he bring me here – was it him?!

2. I can't be sure...

1. You know it was him!

2. Maybe it was...

1. And there was a door I came through...

2. It doesn't open.

1. There's an actual door?!

2. Of course there is...

1. And where is it!?

2. It was easier not seeing the door…

1. Do you know my name?

2. I made myself forget it.

1. Why would you do that!?

2. I don't know why…

1. Do you know your name?

2. None of that's important…!

1 suddenly collapses on the ground and convulses violently.

After ten seconds he stops.

Then –

We don't cry here – we said that once.

1. I know we don't.

A long pause as 2 stands and looks down at him.

Then –

2. There was nothing to start with – and out of that me and you pushed words. (*Slight pause.*) 'Above and there's large clouds looking like islands and through them sunlight shines down – and down on a small town lying by these woods on a hill.' Twenty-seven words I used first.

A pause.

1. 'And in the woods birds caw all manner of noise and drown out the stream that runs through the trees –

As they construct Ballyturk – quiet sounds accompany them.

– and out slowly the stream moves through the town as Ballyturk wakes.'

2. 'And flat terraced houses stand by flat terraced shops – three narrow roads drawn with tarmac and battered by time and rain.'

1. 'And the people of Ballyturk sit on their beds – morning light and radio sounds placing them up and pushing doors and standing out on Moyne Street in clothes stuck with damp and country air. They start.'

During the below the Ballyturk lighting begins to fade back in.

2. And it's Jankie Roller –

1. – and Larry Aspen –

2. – and Cody Finnington –

1. – and Ferdy Oppinton –

2. – and each with their own wants, each with their own skin and voice and each shaped differently – each pushin' their doors open into what's been knitted by us.

The sound of the shop door 'dinging' open.

Hello there, Mrs Drench.

Shattered and 1 can't answer.

Again the sound of the shop door 'dinging' open.

 Hello there, Mrs Drench.

Automatically and 1 slowly walks to the wall and climbs to the high shelf.

Then –

1. Oh hello there, Ferdy. Aren't you lookin' smart for pullin' pints in The Rusty Anchor tonight.

2. Pulln' a kiss from Marnie Reynolds, I hope.

1. And drivin' Larry Aspen green so. Terrible temper on that man – we'll know where that temper will end, Ferdy. In badness, I'd imagine.

A slight pause.

2. I wondered whether you had any lemons, Mrs Drench?

1. I haven't seen a lemon in well over a year I'd say.

2. Oh. And why's that?

1. I won't be out-bittered by a lemon, Ferdy.

2. Bye-bye then.

1 listens to the detailed sounds of Moyne Street all around them now.

Then –

1. Who's making these sounds?

The sounds suddenly stop.

A pause.

2. I'll go to him. It should be me. The eldest should die first.

A slight pause.

1. And what do I do?

A slight pause.

2. Live.

On the floor the alarm clock suddenly starts to sound.

Lights snap to previous as 2 rushes towards it and starts stamping on it.

Suddenly the record player switches itself on and the intro to 'Dancing with Tears in My Eyes' by Ultravox blasts out.

1 goes to the record player, rips up the single and fires it across the space. As it hits the stage-right wall, Nena's '99 Red Balloons' begins to play.

1 flicks through the records and finds that single and flings it at the wall – as it smashes, Survivor's 'Eye of the Tiger' starts to play.

1 flicks through the records and finds it. Furious – he grabs a handful of records and starts smashing them against the stage right wall – unleashing more snippets of eighties classics.

*The four voices on either side of them are heard – the words
from their previous scenes are heard clearly, then spun
backwards and distorted.*

*The pathetic shower suddenly turns itself on – the cuckoo
starts firing in and out of the clock.*

*2 still can't get the alarm off. He's punched it, removed its
innards, swallowed bits of it – but still it's blasting and
getting even louder.*

Blackout but the noise and music continues.

*After four seconds the lights pop back up and 2 jumps out of
the bed.*

*The back wall jolts open two foot and daylight streaks
through.*

*2 looks over at 1 being driven mad by these records/by
everything.*

But this alarm is still sounding.

*2 gathers up all the pieces of the alarm clock and throws
them in the microwave and puts it on.*

He steps back. The microwave explodes.

*1 flings the last record at the wall – Rick Astley's 'Together
Forever' – it shatters and all sounds immediately cut.*

Silence.

Suddenly the cuckoo clock noisily goes on fire.

1 walks slowly towards it – dazed/terrified.

*2 has rushed to a press and takes out a fire extinguisher. He
returns fast to put the fire out but 1 is standing in the way
blocking him.*

1. Let it burn – I can't go on...

*2 fires up the extinguisher, blasting it at the clock and putting
out the fire.*

What is this place!?

2   (*shutting off the fire extinguisher*). Our home.

1. It's not what it was – it's never been what it was…!

2. You'll learn to forget – we did before.

1. A child could forget but not me now!

    A slight pause.

2   (*quietly*). I can't let you die – I won't do that.

1. One walks and one stays talking but either way it's the same death.

    2 smashes 1 in the face, grabs him by the back of the head and talks clearly to him –

2. I'll walk those twelve seconds to him and each step I'll know that you're in here breathing – that'll be all the life I need – d'you understand?

1. Yeah.

    A slight pause.

    Or I think I do – I don't know.

    1 lowers his head. 2 looks at him.

    1 pulls the knife out of the top of the chest of drawers.

    Then –

    There must have been more thoughts on that first day I spent here? Thoughts of parents and maybe brothers and sisters – of another place I lived – a house, a room where I slept and drew pictures – and those memories would have followed me around and outlasted my crying – and maybe I even talked about them – and you of your life as a boy – of course you talked. Maybe you still remembered your life. And we'd listen to each other and time passes quickly and the detail of before, the bad feelings first they fade of course – everything's eaten by the now – by what we build, by what we've become – all this life where Ballyturk appears out of

the darkness and we enter that town as other people shaped
from half-ideas – their houses and streets and trees willed
into life to push us further from what we knew in our
stomachs was real life behind that wall. (*Slight pause.*) How
can I stay here knowing what there is there? How can I talk
about Ballyturk knowing that it's only ever inside this
breaking body and nowhere else? There's no freedom to it –
it's filling rooms with words, not real life... so how?

A pause. He turns and looks at 2 and how broken he looks.

For you I'll stay – 'cause you're more than myself –
whatever that might be. I'll stay.

1 *stares over at his drawings.*

A pause.

A sudden thought –

And maybe knit these words you taught me into something
brand new. Walk us both together in words as the one person.
The wall opens to the outside –

*He places the knife on the table and turns 2 towards his
drawings and stands behind him.*

Music.

– and with your back to me you walk the twelve seconds it
takes to reach him. You walk over the grass and you're a part
of a world full of journeys, the to and fro of small adventure,
of ever-changing pictures and people. There's a stillness in
the breeze out there but each ounce of life is altered by you
now walking in it – you, passed through the air and out over
countryside, over what must be oceans and part of the
texture of real life now. You're there in the grass and
stretched out in trees and made alive by day and spun in
colours too heartbreaking to mention. Land and sea holding
each other and holding upon it these people carried along by
heartbeat and dreams of love and talking to one another and
waking with one another and planning uncertain futures that
are free, that have possibility as you do now in these twelve
seconds that you walk –

1 *covers his own eyes and really tries to be there.*

– and each step walked away from what was taken from us, what was wasted and stolen by something other than us – and a step right now brings chance, a breath can fill with hope, where a boy can feel the sun on his face and throw open a door and run in a day dusted in not just the word 'beach' but the beach itself – while another boy walks in a countryside forever free and talking endlessly to a sister – talking stupidly.

2 *turns to look at him.*

You walk from this room and your spirit, past and present, wraps with the spirit of billions of others, and it's this that invisibly holds up this planet of ours in space – in brilliant openness – in freedom. You walk away quietly.

1 *lowers his hands and sees* 2 *looking at him.*

And it must be happiness you feel – and what you're walking towards is forgotten – or if remembered it holds no fear this 'death'. (*Slight pause.*) You're a lived person and in those twelve seconds you're a part of the world – you've stared at a life and walked in it and it's all the life you need. It's real. Real life.

Suddenly the wall begins to open out – but this time there is no mechanical noise –

– it is the imagined quiet elemental sounds of the Earth heard from our troposphere – of winds, oceans, nature, of us.

The wall opens and the evening light is beautiful out there – and on the small hill, little marigold flowers have grown in the grass.

1 *and* 2 *look towards it.*

On the hill and 3 *is seated behind an office desk, waiting for his dead.*

The wall lands softly on the grass.

Then –

2. Go on.

For a beat – 1 is unsure what's been said.

Go.

1 turns away and walks from the room and into life.

It's 2 who stays. He covers his eyes.

1 walks in the outside through the world – for twelve seconds he's free.

3 stands up from his seat to meet him.

The wall rises again.

All sounds cut as the wall closes and shuts 2 back into the room.

He takes his hands away from his eyes and stands alone in the silence for some moments.

He doesn't know what to do.

He slowly turns around and looks at his cell.

He stares at 1's drawings on the walls. He walks closer and closer to the stage-left wall – and stops a foot away from a drawing.

The cuckoo clock sounds three times. He turns and looks blankly at it.

Suddenly there's a knocking from the stage-right wall. Instinctively 2 picks up the knife from the table.

The knocking more desperate now as 2 walks towards a chest of drawers. It's coming from behind there.

In one movement he moves back the furniture fast.

Behind there the wall is moving – a small door has been wallpapered over – someone is trying to get in.

2 quickly shoves the knife into the wall and cuts around the door – which reaches four foot in height.

He stops and stands back.

Very slowly the door opens inwards.

A long pause.

A seven-year-old GIRL *enters dressed in leggings, runners and a sweatshirt.*

Lost and frightened she stares at 2 – expecting him to hurt her.

Music.

Behind her the little door closes shut.

Feeling no threat from 2 – the GIRL *turns and looks at the room as the music swells.*

2 turns and looks out.

His eyes slowly close.

Blackout.

The End – the music continuing in darkness.